ZERO IDENTITY

Per

Maxwell Mendes Oliveira

November 2015.

More than special thanks:

For my wife Michelli Aparecida Maranho and my little daughter Maria Júlia.

For my parents Mauro and Vilmar.

For my brother of letters, Gamma .

One

The door was unlocked as expected. Ricardo was there, sprawled on the couch, drunk, drugged, or both. He approached him. Ricardo didn't even look in her direction. She took the weapon she was carrying, put it in his hand, which was not showing any reaction. He brought Ricardo's hand with the gun up to his chin. He pressed his finger on the trigger. Brains flew back.

She left the gun there, in his hand. He looked once more at the scene

before him and left the apartment.

That night, Tomás looked out of the hotel room window once more. He stared at the street. He thought of Eliana, her sweet gaze, her smooth white skin, her natural scent. Tomás had an intimate joke that she didn't even need to apply soap, it already had natural perfume.

Did she have to marry that guy? The son of a bitch was so pissed off too, he pressed on, showing that he was the best match, that she had no choice but to marry him. And as for him, Tomás, there was nothing to say.

He had, at the time they were dating, lost an immense fortune in a disastrous investment. He didn't have a penny, nothing, not even a cat to pull his tail as they said inside.

Eliana wasn't at fault, couldn't blame her. After all, Tomás knew he couldn't give her anything, anything she deserved. Ricardo, on the contrary. Big, rich farmer father. Playboy full of tribal tattoos, with Big of the Year in the garage. Everything he couldn't give.

Tomás went to the bathroom, washed his face, went back to the bedroom. He lay down on the bed. I had to take a bus the other day.

The descent from Curitiba was always calm . Despite the mountain having a fucked up movement, due to the flow of trucks going to the ports of Paranaguá and Antonina, Tomás always enjoyed the trip. The bouncing of the bus even gave her a little sleep.

	The trip to Curitiba had been a work commitment that had turned into a great occasion. She was working in a store. He thought about going in, but stopped hesitantly. It would end up scaring her. But maybe I would never get another chance, who knows. He went back to the store and talked to her. As it was close to lunch time, they went to a mall.

She was still beautiful, her smile as always radiating that sweetness. When he hugged her, Tomás felt the softness of her skin again. They sat at one of the tables in the food court.

- So, tell me about yourself, how's it going? she asked as they sat down.

- Ah, I got a job at an importer. I work as a logistics analyst. Recovering from that "financial tumble" of years ago. Is that you?

Eliana broke her smile, lowered her head to the tabletop a moment before answering. When she looked up again, Thomas noticed that her eyes were watering.

- I regretted having married Tomás. I shouldn't have left

you. Ricardo is a disappointment. His father died a while ago , I think you knew. Since then, he's been destroying his share of the inheritance. Now he's using drugs, he doesn't go a day without using them. He's already ended up with a good part of the money his father left him. We have the apartment and some finances because I made him leave it in my name.

"To support his addiction, he's already sold a lot of things, he doesn't give a penny at home. I was the one who had to take this job in a store to support him. And when I talk to him, the fool only know how to laugh, acting as a mentally retarded , stopped sitting on the couch like a madman. "

She told a little more about Ricardo's stupidities. Tomás was listening to everything. That filled him with hatred, but he didn't want to show it, it wasn't going to disturb her outburst.

"I would like to help you," he said, putting his hand over hers.

Eliana showed her smile again.

- You being here is a very good thing.

Two

The bus arrived at the bus station. Tomás took a taxi that left him at the door of his building. He climbed the stairs to the second floor, where he lived. He took a quick shower, changed into more comfortable clothes. He went to the fridge, got a cold beer, sat on the couch.

The touch of Eliana's hand on his still had the power to move him, as nothing else had. It was incandescent. He recalled the last moments he spent with her at the mall before they said goodbye:

- I miss you so much. It's a confusion of feelings - she said, after a few moments of silence.

- So it is. I think still, it's a good thing you didn't pick me right away, I would have taken both of us to the hole too. And I would have felt terrible if that had happened.

- Do not blame yourself. Nobody can imagine that an investment that looked so good would sink and take a lot of people with it. You, at least, are getting up, got a job, are getting back on track. And Ricardo? Ricardo doesn't want anything to do with anything. A woman needs to feel secure about her man. And I need to feel that way.

Tomás shook her hand, with as much affection as possible. As if he could retain that contact.

- Let him go, stay with me - he said, unable to control the flood of words.

- I have a Thomas wedding, an engagement. I love you so much. You made me feel wonderful today, but I have an appointment. Let's just enjoy this little time together, okay?

He was forced to agree. She was right, and more than right, she had respect for commitment, which Ricardo didn't. When they said goodbye, she approached him and whispered in his ear:

- Don't forget me anymore, please.

In which he replied:
- Never.
He handed her a card with his cell phone number on it. I told her I could call her when she needed to.
Back in the present and in his apartment, Tomás was still remembering her profile walking as she walked away from him. Should he have tried to win her back before she married him? Maybe he never knew.
Trying to dispel his thoughts, Tomás finished his beer. He turned on the television. The police news was running at that moment. He always thought the police news was getting more and more bloodthirsty. The presenter, a

journalist (if he could be called that) from a radio show, fired off his flamboyant chatter:

- Man found dead indoors. Police work with a suicide hypothesis. Attention, it has just arrived for me here on the spot, the dead man's name is Ricardo Pasternack , from a very rich family here in the capital.

Tomás leaned forward at that moment. Her heart seemed to leap into her mouth. The journalist continued:

- Yesterday, around six o'clock, the wife arrived at the apartment where they lived, and found her husband dead with a gunshot to the head. In the dead man's hand, an automatic.

"According to neighbors, the boy was a drug user, and his wife has been keeping the house accounts. That's what I say: as long as they don't put an end to this damn drug, and all the drug dealers, many wives, mothers and fathers, will mourn the death of their husbands and children. You have to stop this crap now".

Tomás turned off the TV. As if answering a thought of his, the cell phone rang at that exact moment. It was Eliana:

- Hi, Tomás, it's me.

- Hi, I just saw it on the news. Why didn't you call me just yesterday? I would have come back," he said, worried.

- It's all right. The police chief said that they didn't steal anything, that they found drugs in his body, there was even some in his nose. My God, Thomas, I've never seen so much blood.

- I'll take the first bus and go up, I'll meet you there quickly - he said, already getting up.

- No my dear, don't worry. I'll take care of releasing his body, then burying him. I just need to know you're there. It helps me a lot, already this way.

- I am always here.

At that moment, although it was not the most favorable for that, but Tomás felt like the happiest man in the world.

Three

Tomás practically worked on autopilot that week. He called Eliana practically every day after he returned from work at the importer. She said that police work was merely a formality. According to her, the officer told him that the investigation c onfirmaram that Ricardo was just a drug addict who had reached the limits of the disease. The act of taking one's own life was simply the only way to get rid of the addiction. It was kind of complicated.

"Perhaps, deep down, it was his only gesture of manhood,"

she commented, as they chatted on her cell phone.

- And do you think the police will take a while to finish the investigation?

- I don't know, and I don't worry too much about it. In fact, I don't even want to think about it too much. And you, what do you tell me?

- Working and getting mad at not being able to be near you.

- Tomás, understand my dear. I just lost my husband. I have to mourn. People might think it's cool, but I was raised in the countryside, and I respect that a lot. You understand me?

- Of course, I understand yes. But when it passes

remember that I'll be here, right?

She gave a discreet and pleasant laugh over the phone.

- I know you do. Now I need to hang up. A kiss dear, we'll talk tomorrow.

- Other. I will be waiting for you.

Once the phone was moved, Thomas put it on the coffee table. He leaned back on the couch, his eyes fixed on the ceiling. He wondered if Eliana would like to live there. It was a small, simple apartment. He did not live in the capital, although the city was very good. She had a life there, had a world of her.

He, Tomás, in turn, had no friends, no life. After he lost all the money, his friends abandoned him. It was discreetly, one after the other. *Nice bunch of bastards*, he thought. He sat down on the sofa.

It was time to continue. He went to the bathroom, took a good shower. He put on new clothes. He took his wallet, cell phone, apartment keys and left. On the lips, a discreet smile.

Beach Street at the time of Square July 29. I walked hurriedly by cobblestone street. The sound of his shoes echoing on the street stones. I looked at the people around, as those who do

not care about anything, as nonchalantly. It was when he saw. He followed her as discreetly as possible. She had just left work, a restaurant in which it already had lunch a few times. They were getting close to a bus stop. The approach could not be too abrupt, not his intention to frighten her.

He approached her, that's when she turned her head back, noticing his presence. Stopped.

- Hi, you around here? – was all she said.

- Yeah, I was passing by, that's when I saw you.

She smiled.

- What are you doing now? he asked nonchalantly.
- I was going to take the bus home.
- Do you wanna a ride? My car is close by.
She stumbled. With the excuse to take a shortcut, followed by a narrow alleyway. There was not time to react. He struck her in the head and at the time of the back using an iron pipe that carried hidden, with all possible force.

<u>bedroom</u>

Tomás got up that Sunday as if he had been beaten up. A

tired body, a sign of a bad night's sleep. He took a shower, changed his clothes, went down the stairs and went to the square near the building where he lived. He stopped at a newsstand where he bought two newspapers. Then he went to the bakery where he used to go . He bought French breads, cheese buns and a piece of pineapple cake, one of his favorites. He was ravaged by hunger. He went home, made the coffee. He ate a little of everything and went to the sofa in the living room, lie down and read the newspaper.

Lazy little Sunday morning , he thought as he flipped through the paper.

He was brought out of his peace by the sound of his cell phone. It was Eliana.

"Hi, sorry if I woke you up," she said, her voice anxious.

- No, I was reading the newspaper here in the living room. What happened? You look scared.

- It's just that I read here in the newspaper that something happens, and that left me very shocked.

- What was it?

- An ex-lover of Ricardo's, she died. The newspaper spoke of robbery followed by death. I think it's robbery they talk about, isn't it?

- Yes. But Eliana, what is this ex-lover story ?

- You live in her town.

- Is she from around here? Eliana, explain this to me correctly, I don't understand anything.

- Sorry Tomás, I'm so nervous I shuffled everything. Can you come here?

- I can. Hang in there, I'll be there in a couple of hours.

- Thank you, thank you.

Tomás passed through the building's entrance hall. It was hard to believe that Ricardo was detonating the heritage by living in a building like that. The porter, who had already been warned, let him in on his own. Entering the elevator, he pressed the button for her floor. When he played the campaign from her apartment, and Eliana opened the door, he could see how much she had been crying. She hugged him before he could say anything. Tomás let her stay like that for a few moments (also because he was enjoying hugging her) before speaking:

- Calm down, what happened?

Eliana indicated a sofa. They sat down. She had some newspapers on a coffee table.

- I went to buy my newspaper when I saw the news. She was murdered Tomás, in her city. And I think the blame is mine.

- Like this? Eliana, you're not talking thing to thing. Who is this person?

She handed him a newspaper. Tomás read the article: *On this Saturday night, around 8 pm, in the city of Paranaguá, 22-year-old Evangelina de Souza was found dead. The victim was a waitress at the Prato Fino restaurant. According to early information, it is believed that the criminal intended to steal her, as her bag was found at the scene of the crime, all overturned. Still, according to the police, there was no sexual violence, the victim was killed with a severe blow to the skull. So far, no suspects have been found"*.

Tomás vaguely remembered having read

something similar in Paranaguá's newspapers.

- That was Ricardo's lover? he asked, after putting the newspaper on the coffee table.

- Yes. And I am guilty of her death, Tomás.

- What do you mean Eliana? Guilty how?

- I wished she died.

Four

Tomás gave him a glass of water. Eliana drank in long gulps. After she was done, she placed the glass on the little table. He sat down beside her and gently took her hand.
   - Tell me now, what is this crazy story? he asked , as gently as possible.
   - This Evangelina was Ricardo's lover before we got married. She hit on him directly, while we were dating, in front of me . She lived around here, looks like she was an executive secretary. On the eve of us getting married, I told him, or me, or her. He chose to

be with me. The woman even tried to talk to him, but I went after her and gave her a good slap. I hit so hard that she fell to the ground. And I said loud and clear that if she went after him again, I would kill her. And now, she dies two weeks after him.

    Tomás put his arm gently around her shoulders, pulled her close to him.

    - That's it, you didn't do anything. Feeling guilty because someone died, without you having done anything, has nothing to do with it. In fact, the police themselves are thinking it was robbery.

    - I know, but I feel a little guilty yes Tomás, you know, I think there is a lot in my head. And now, Júnior, Ricardo's brother goes around saying that he thinks he didn't commit suicide, that it was murder.

- Hey, but this one is new. And what did the police say?

- They didn't say anything, but Junior still thinks it was murder. You are willing to pay for private expertise and all. The thing is, I don't know if that's going to happen or not. The marshal seemed pretty sure it was suicide. He thinks Junior's story is too absurd. He is dying to call the investigations closed.

- Well, if he's suspecting something, look into it then.

- Yes, but he is also getting involved in the case of Evangelina.

- Like this? What exactly does one crime have to do with another?

- Evangelina, before becoming Ricardo's lover, was his girlfriend. I think Junior is angry and wants to punish someone.

- So you don't have to blame yourself. If he is in remorse, anger, pain, or whatever it is that resolves. I think you're more of a victim for all the suffering you've carried than they are.

- I should have married you yourself Tomás - she said, looking at him.

- I had just lost money, I couldn't make you happy.

- Not for the money, you would have made me happy anyway. You would have taken great care of me.

He tenderly stroked her face. Their eyes met deeply at that moment.

They kissed slowly, delighting in each other.

Five

Tomás looked out the window, it had been raining for a week. It looked like everyone was going to be a frog. It had also been a week since he had met Eliana. A week since the kiss. The desire to talk to her again was great. The phone rang at that moment. Was her.
- Hi, I was thinking about you now - he said, a huge smile on his lips.
- I was also thinking of you. Miss you my love. But I have to tell you something ridiculous and boring that happened.
- What was it?

- I went out with some friends from the service, when I looked in the rearview mirror of the car and saw a car following me. I didn't say anything to them. Well, we stopped at a restaurant with a beautiful terrace, we were eating, drinking a beer, when I looked out over the balcony and saw the same car parked next to mine. There ready, after all that has happened these past few days, I was paranoid . I spoke with a friend of mine who is the girlfriend of a civil police officer. She asked her boyfriend to stop by and check it out. Her boyfriend came with his colleague. They gave the guy a press. We ended up at the police station. Guess the outcome.

- This is Eliana, I'm getting purple with worry.

- The guy was a private detective. He was hired by my dearest brother-in-law, Junior. He said that my brother-in-law wanted to know exactly what I was doing, what I had done the day Ricardo died. Can such a thing as Tomás?

- But what is this nonsense about this guy? And what did the detective say? That your brother-in-law suspects both of us?

- No, he suspects me. You think I had Ricardo killed. So he convinced the chief (I believe he even threatened the poor man with a lawsuit) to listen to me again. And I mentioned you in my statement. They will want to hear you too.

- No problem. That brother-in-law of yours is a figure, huh?

- And you don't know which is worse. He even sent the detective to see if there was any connection with Evangelina's death. The detective explained that he went down there in Paranaguá, but as far as he found out, he concluded that he had no relationship at all.

- In other words, the asshole wants to assign me one more kill?

- Well, it's love, sorry about that whole roll.

Love, she called me love, thought Tomás.

- Don't worry, when will they want to hear from me?
- I think soon.
- No problem, I'll go, and see you there.
- I'll love it.
- Me too.

Six

Thomas looked at the clock. I was waiting for forty-five minutes. The police station was just like other public offices that had visited. From time to time, police passed, sometimes alone, in pairs, and sometimes bringing a "guest" handcuffed, as would his grandfather, who was a fan of a former police radio program.

Eliana was still inside the police chief's office, accompanied by her lawyer, a tall, thin man with gray hair and heavy gold-rimmed glasses named dr. Butter. When he greeted him, the man showed a firm, strong handshake. He also saw the face of Ricardo's brother, the Junior guy. His full name, Tomás later learned, was Aureliano Gonçalves Pasternack Júnior. It was an almost perfect replica of Ricardo, only fatter and looking like a dead fish. He entered with Eliana. Finally the office door opened. The clerk appeared:

- Mister Tomás, can you come in, please?

Tomás promptly entered the office. The place looked more like the living room of some middle-class apartment than the working environment of a public servant. There was a sofa in one corner, a hack with a LED TV, which showed a pay TV channel, in the other corner, a table with a computer and printer, where the clerk was sitting. In the center, the desk with the police chief's personal computer. Eliana was sitting on the sofa accompanied by her lawyer. He gave a discreet smile. In the other corner, Junior watched impassively.

The sheriff was a thin man with black curly hair. He wore a short-sleeved shirt.

- Good afternoon, Tomás. Sit down, please - he asked, indicating a chair for him.

Tomás thanked him and sat down.

- Please give your full name, address and RG number.

Tomás informed.

- What can you tell about the day of Mr. Ricardo Pasternack 's death ? asked the chief, starting the interrogation.

- Well, I had come here in the capital to deal with some business for the firm when I passed in front of the store where Dona Eliana worked. As she is an old friend, I called her to talk. During her lunch break, we went to a mall, had something to eat, had a beer. We talked for a while and each one went to his side. I left the other day.

- And what did you talk about?

- About the direction of our lives. I said I was working at an importer, she said she was working in a store and was still married.

- Did she say anything about the wedding?

- Yes. She said that her husband was a drug addict, that he had spent a good part of his inheritance on his addiction.

At that moment, did Junior speak?

- Of course you're counting like that. You're wanting to protect this "little one" - he said, being interrupted by a gesture from the chief.

- Señor Aureliano, Sr. Junior. Be quiet there, okay? You are watching the deposition only because your lawyer, who is a good friend of ours, asked me to. If you say anything else, I'll tell you to leave.

Junior returned to his quiet place. Tomás' testimony continued for a while longer. The delegate dictated the terms to the clerk, and soon afterward Tomás signed. All were dismissed. Outside the police station, Eliana and Tomás said goodbye to her lawyer. He stayed to see another customer. Out on the street, Eliana breathed a sigh of relief.

- Look, if we had rehearsed, it wouldn't have turned out so good. The lawyer, dr. Butter, he liked it a lot - she commented.

- Yeah, but your brother-in-law didn't like it very much.

- Don't care. Junior is just trying to prove something he's not. You should have seen it, I said the exact same thing. Junior didn't say anything in my statement, but I could see that he was very upset.
  - I think he really thinks we killed Ricardo and this Evangelina.
  - I'll leave you at the railroad my love, is that today, I have a lot of work in the store.
  - All right. See you later.

Seven

Tomás got up from the bed with a start. A knocking sound at the door woke him. Who could it be how you got into the building? he asked himself, rising from the bed.

He walked into the living room. He looked through the peephole, only to see a figure in the hallway. More insistent knocks. Tomás opened the door. The first punch hit him in the left eye. He felt his head thrown back. The second was in the belly. He bent forward. Then he felt a strong but not blunt blow on the back of his head. He felt two strong hands drag him to an armchair in the corner of the room. When he managed to open his eyes, Junior's face appeared before him. He was still expressionless, but this time he had an automatic in his right hand.

- So, son of a bitch, are you ready to answer my questions? – he said, his voice ominously calm .

- What you want?

- Answer me: was it you, that bitch or the two who killed my brother and Evangelina?

- None of us.

- Don't lie to me, I 'm serious. If I get really angry, I'll kill you.

Tomás felt around on the coffee table beside his chair.

- And do you think I would lie to a guy who has a gun that size in his hand?

- Of course you would lie. And do you want to know what I think? Eliana's bitch told you to and you just carried out the orders to kill them both. Tell the truth man.

Found it , thought Tomás, squeezing the cheap crystal ashtray.

- Think well Junior: wasn't it easier for me to catch Eliana and for her to separate from her brother?

- It would be, but she should want him out of her life forever.

- You just forgot one thing: the private detective that you hired yourself, testified to the police, saying he didn't find anything against me or her.

- I just don't know how you managed to fool the guy, but I know you did.

Junior brought his face close to Tomás's this time.

- Tell me the truth, will you? Then you suffer less.

The whole thing unfolded quickly. Tomás hit Junior's left forehead with the crystal ashtray. This one got a little dizzy. The two began to fight for the weapon. Tomás was almost able to take the gun from the other's hand when they reached the window. Afterwards, all she remembered was that the two of them had rushed past her and fallen towards the parking lot. Tomás remembered that he lived on the second floor.

Shit , was his last thought before he blacked out.

- Hey, young man, are you alright? - Said a voice, coming from far, far away.

Thomas opened his eyes. A policeman was standing beside him. What was funny was that he, Tomás, was lying down. And the policeman was almost at his height. It was when, trying to get up, that he realized he was lying on top of a car. He remembered Junior.

- And or another, where is it? he asked, his voice a whisper with pain.

- You talk about the crazy guy with the gun?

- Yes.

- He died. It is now being taken to the IML. He fell face first on the pavement. Head trauma at the time.

Eight

Thomas opened his eyes. It was at night. It took a while for his eyes to get used to the darkness. The infirmary room was white, immaculately white. On a sofa in the corner, he noticed a figure. It was Eliana.

- You have to rest love. The doctor said you were very lucky," she said, waking up instantly and approaching the bed.

- Yeah, if I lived on the third floor, I don't think I would have survived.

Eliana patted his face.

- Now it's over. The delegate from Curitiba informed my lawyer that he did not find any evidence of a crime in Ricardo's death, so he closed the case. And as for Júnior, the police here only want to take his statement later, just to confirm what they had already discovered: that Junior was crazy.

- And when will he take my statement? I say the delegate here?

- As soon as you can get out of the hospital. The doctor said that by the end of the week you can leave.

- And my boss, what will he tell me about it? I will probably be fired.

- Don't worry, I'm sure he'll understand. I'll talk to him tomorrow.
- You stayed with me the whole time?
- I would stay with you forever.
- Will you marry me?
- I want.

- I'm glad you're better Mr Tomás and you can give your testimony - said the police chief, indicating a chair for him.

The Paranaguá police station operated in a building a little older than the one in the capital. The office was much more like that of a police chief.

- For me it's great that you can take my testimony soon. I

want to sort this out soon and get back to my life as normal.

  Tomás promptly gave his testimony, which the delegate dictated to the clerk. He explained everything that had happened, from the moment he opened the door to the moment he and Junior threw themselves out the window. As soon as he finished, the delegate thanked him and dismissed him. When he went out into the street, he took out his cell phone and called Eliana's number.

  - Honey, I left the police station. It was all right. According to the delegate, my testimony matched what had been found. I'm going home.

- Wow, I'm dead - said Eliana, finishing taking off her wedding dress.

A month had passed since Junior's attack. She and Tomás were surprised how quickly the police handled everything. The delegate concluded that Júnior, in a fit of madness, decided to blame Tomás and Eliana for the deaths of Ricardo and Evangelina.

While Tomás helped Eliana out of her dress, he touched her bare shoulder.

"You can't imagine how long I've been waiting for this," he muttered.

Eliana turned to him. He had an enigmatic smile on his face.

- I want to ask you something.
- He speaks.
- Now that I am your legitimate wife, we are accomplices, no matter what happens. I know you killed them both. It just confirms me.

"Yes," he replied, after a moment of silence.

They looked deeply into each other's eyes.

- You killed them for me?
- Yes, you know that. I love you.

She kissed him on the mouth.

"I love you too," she whispered.

Nine

They were seated at a table by the hotel pool. The honeymoon was taking place in a hotel in Bahia. Tomás took a sip of his cold drink. Since the wedding night, when he confessed what he had done, they hadn't mentioned it again. They made love, slept, and got ready to travel. Now, here, maybe it was time to talk about it.

Eliana, who was lying on the deck chair beside him, on her stomach, letting the sun burn her back, turned to him.

- Are you wanting to talk about that subject? she said,

her eyes hidden behind her glasses.

- Yes.

- Tell me, how did you manage to do everything so well?

- I already knew almost everything about your life. I had hired a private detective to let me know how you were. He informed me of everything: d rogas, his involvement with Evangelina, everything. I had a damned hatred for him.

"All I had to do was sneak into your building. I entered through the garage. I went up to your floor. On the fire escape, I put on a different outfit that I had in a backpack, put on rubber gloves I had bought at a drugstore, went into his apartment. He left the door open. I walked into the living room. He was so drunk and drugged that he didn't say anything, didn't even seem to notice that someone was there. I took the gun, put it in his hand and squeezed his finger on the trigger."

- And why Evangelina? she asked, sitting down on the lounge chair.

- Well, as I told you, I already knew about that whole thing between him and her, before he married you. And as she had come to Paranaguá, I found out that she worked in a restaurant near her home. I went to the restaurant a few times to see her up close. We even talked trivialities a few times.

"So I just followed her one night. She saw me, smiled, and I offered her a ride in a car that didn't exist. She accompanied me. I gave her a hard knock or two on the head, rummaged through her purse, took her money and left. Police still think robbery was Alías ".

- And as for Junior, was it self-defense, or did you really kill him?

- No, he really wanted to kill me. Punched me a couple of times. The rest you already know.

- Did you know that you are a man without equal? – she said, sitting on his lap.

- Like this?

- You did for me, what no man would ever do for a woman. Love you.
- Me too.